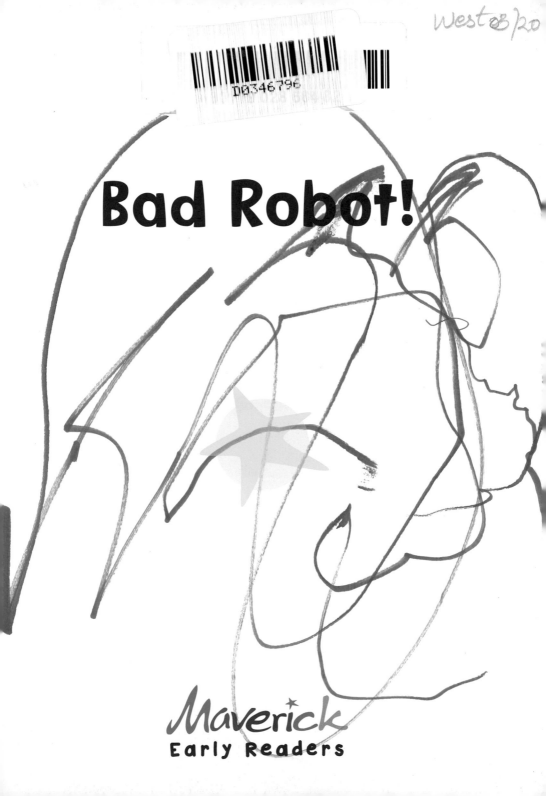

Bad Robot!

Maverick
Early Readers

'Bad Robot!'
An original concept by Elizabeth Dale
© Elizabeth Dale

Illustrated by Felicia Whaley

Published by MAVERICK ARTS PUBLISHING LTD

Studio 11, City Business Centre, 6 Brighton Road,

Horsham, West Sussex, RH13 5BB

© Maverick Arts Publishing Limited February 2020

+44 (0)1403 256941

A CIP catalogue record for this book is available at the British Library.

ISBN 978-1-84886-659-1

Maverick
pub
www.maverickbooks.co.uk

Yellow

This book is rated as: Yellow Band (Guided Reading)
This story is mostly decodable at Letters and Sounds Phase 3.
Up to eight non-decodable story words are included.

Bad Robot!

by **Elizabeth Dale**

illustrated by
Felicia Whaley

Rob is Max's robot.

Rob gets the washing in.

No, Rob! Stop!

The washing is not dry yet.

But Rob will not stop!

Then he tips up the bin.

But Rob will not stop!

14

He kicks the rubbish.

Mum gets crosser and crosser.

17

Max is sad. So is Rob.

Then Rob sees Mum's ring.

Look, it is raining.

The washing has not got wetter,

thanks to Rob.

You are such a good robot. You must not go.

Quiz

1. What does Rob get in?
a) The cat
b) Max
c) The washing

2. Why is Mum cross?
a) Rob stops
b) Rob will not stop
c) Max makes a mess

3. Rob _____ the rubbish.
a) Flips
b) Kicks
c) Helps

4. What does Rob see in the rubbish?
a) The washing
b) Max's toy
c) Mum's ring

5. At the end, what is Rob?
a) A good robot
b) A washing robot
c) A bad robot

Turn over for answers

Book Bands for Guided Reading

The Institute of Education book banding system is a scale of colours that reflects the various levels of reading difficulty. The bands are assigned by taking into account the content, the language style, the layout and phonics. Word, phrase and sentence level work is also taken into consideration.

Maverick Early Readers are a bright, attractive range of books covering the pink to white bands. All of these books have been book banded for guided reading to the industry standard and edited by a leading educational consultant.

To view the whole Maverick Readers scheme, visit our website at

www.maverickearlyreaders.com

Or scan the QR code above to view our scheme instantly!

Quiz Answers: 1c, 2b, 3b, 4c, 5a

Pink
Red
Yellow
Blue
Green
Orange
Turquoise
Purple
Gold
White